The Brixcity A.C.T

Cordell Charles

Contact Us:
TheAoi.ESCorp@gmail.com
TheAoi.US@gmail.com

To order additional copies of this book, contact:
Xlibris
844-714-8691
www.Xlibris.com
Orders@Xlibris.com

ISBN: Softcover   978-1-6698-7948-0
        Hardcover   978-1-6698-7947-3
        EBook   978-1-6698-7949-7

Library of Congress Control Number: 2023910303

Print information available on the last page

Rev. date: 11/20/2023

Created By AOI

Art of Innovation

Written By: **Cordell Charles**

Presented By AES

TaBle of Contents

The Hystalorian: AWON

Burthing Territory, Septum – 22 years ago,

Septum's Plunge, ...a huge waterfall that would eventually go on to become known to all as "The Great Plunge." This was before the creation of the coveted cups and the revival of our monarchy. So, soon was the day that the myths of lore came for us. Their arrival would cause unimaginable events, leading us into a time of era that would reshape the very fabrics of our known world. It was here, on The Great Plunge, that sparked the beginning of the end and 'A World Of New' for mankind . . . in historic fashion.

Everyone in the known world knew they were coming, but what they didn't know was the level of chaos and destruction that they would be bringing with them. An irrefutable clash of wills, one that would completely change our society as we knew it. A mythical war, slowly made its way to the shores of Penyow, and with it 'Dojakai'.

According to the Father of Dojakai, who honors us with echoes from his accounts of the Mythocolypes. . .

"It was complete madness up there I'll tell you that. There was so much chaos, so much destruction. The Dojakai weren't only attacking us, they were attacking each other as well. Some were . . . There seemed to have been factions of sorts, yeah. This was an old war, their war. We people had just gotten caught up in the middle of it. Before 'The Infamous AD Venture', no one even knew of the existence of Dojakai. And yet, had the Amazin' Eights as a whole not been there, in the trenches of this great Dojakai war, surely we-all would not be here to talk about this today. As you know, we lost one of our best on the plunge that day. The Amazin Howla, it or not he was the real hero . . . never to be forgotten . . . It was said that we should welcome Dojakai as a sign from the stars now more than ever. I know, I was the last man standing, but it was the will of Howla that saved the day, not mine. In the end, regardless of your belief in Dojakai. Be them our annihilators or our saviors, one fact now remains, whether you like them or not, the truth is we are no longer alone in this world. Dojakai are here to stay, overcoming your bias will help you all accept that the world simply will not and can not ever be the same as we once knew it. And I for one am okay with that, and anyone whose anyone should respect that. That's all I have for now, with great honor of my own, Long Live Amazin Eights, Cheers." IV Cool is quoted saying.

Welcome to the world of DojaKai . . .

READY UP

...Luka's house, present day,

"**I** don't even know when it happens sometimes, I can't like, make it happen, d'you know what I mean," Luka narrates. "All I know is that when it does happen, I feel . . . kinda invincible. Like, I don't feel bad here. I don't feel fear here or any other emotions that makes me feel less than myself. The only thing I can feel is this adoring rush. The slight sensation of what feels like a spark of electricity radiating through my bones or this feeling of invisible flames crashing over my skin like waves, only it's in the form of a cool breeze. Everything is heightened. I am as tough as steel. I am faster than sound. I can feel the pressure of my blood pushing through my body, it's warm but somehow it's as cold as ice and yet still my muscles are on fire, as hot as the soaring sun. There's this explosion of energy that starts in the pit of my stomach, traveling throughout every corner of my body. My eyes are open, but I am in complete darkness, yet somehow I can see everything so much clearer. I know it sounds like nonsense and yeah, yeah, it's all in my head, but it can feel more real than reality sometimes. No one who's seen me like this knows what to make of it. "Daydreams," Dad calls it, and today was no different. It was just your average and calm peaceful day—the perfect day to lock in and focus on my warm-ups actually—but that's usually when it always happens, when I lose myself. First starts the faint cheers from a restless crowd, which eventually turns into soft rumbles and then it begins to build little by little until finally a roaring chant becomes clear to the ear, as clear as the deep pounding of oxygen pumping blood into in my chest," Luka narrates as we take in the beautiful scene.

"Luka! Luka! Luka! Luka! Luka!" A crowd suddenly explodes.

"I understand my assignment.." Luka narrates. "Beat my opponent into blissful unconsciousness. Something I've yet to actually accomplish outside of my head, if I'm being technical. But here in my domain, the place where I am king, here in my temples, I have beaten many, some even twice my size. It's dark here, but I can see everything that's happening as clear as this day. My actual vision becomes like windows to reality, like an illustrious interactive backdrop that I could careless about, which somehow can still be seen from inside the safety of my temples. I can see movements in my real-time backdrop but sometimes I ignore things the more drunk I become from the roaring excitement of the crowd in my head. After a while nothing else matters to me, but the glory of the win I am sure to receive once the clashing begins. I think I scared dad when I told him it's like being in two realities at the same time. It's shocking to most how vividly I can dream, but I don't know, I find it high-key interesting," Luka narrates.

...In actual reality, Andrew steps off of the front porch and into the yard, holding not far from Luka. He looks down, picking from a small pile of marbled stones by his feet. Luka is just standing there with a blank expression, completely ignorant to his father's presence. That, is because in his head, the fight has already popped off.

Ready up: Scene

...Inside Luka's imagination,

"Oh!! He cracked him! He cracked him! That's it! That punch laid him out! I don't believe it! That guy is blissfully unconscious! And once again the crowd favorite Luka! Has indeed actually done it! That was one for the Hystalorian people," explains the speculator.

"Ladies and gentlemen! Your esteemed winner and new! Monarch is—" An announcer calls in his firmest voice.

A shadowed figure jumps out of the crowd, pauses for a bit then begins running at Luka.

"Ayo, wait, hold on. Who's this now? Is this a new challenger? Why didn't I know about this? Where did he even come from?" The spectator says while looking through pages in front of him. "Two years in the making, and this is the outcome. Aw Myths help us." The speculator says off-air of the microphone. "Hey, somebody, stop him, Stop that guy!"

The mysterious man incased in shadows is running right at Luka. His face isn't yet visible in the shadow but he is wearing a red metal belt sash, red leather gloves and a skintight bodysuit made of an indescribable material. In that instant, Andrew can be seen preparing himself on the big screen above from a projector within Luka's imagination. Luka is too distracted by the mysterious man to notice what's happening in reality as projected on the Jumbotron. Andrew tosses the stone up and catches it a few times sizing it's weight and feel in his hands before heaving it at Luka's head. On the Jumbotron it shoots at the camera with tremendous force, so hard it actually whistles through the air like it had been shot from a cannon.

Ready up: Scene

...Back in front of Luka's house–in actual reality,

"Oh no, kid, look out!" the speculator yells from inside the head of Luka.

Luke glances up at the big screen at the same time as the mystery man's fist and the small rock pitched by Andrew connects with Luka's face, cracking him perfectly between the eyes. The pebble takes him off his feet, he quickly grabs the bridge of his nose with both hands falling head first on to his neck. 'Reality hurts'. He hits the floor pretty hard releasing an unintentional groan. Suddenly he snaps out of his daydream, immediately pops open his eyes and sits up realizing where he actually is. The first thing he sees is his father's intense face glaring at him. Luka cringes like he sees a ghost then quickly releases a huge goofy smile not before standing up. He scratches his head while cocking it to the side cheesing as hard as he possibly can, trying desperately to lighten his father's murderous glare.

"Eeeee–A-hehe . ., uh, hiya, Dad, I didn't see you walk up–what a sunny day huh?," Luka says nervously...

Andrew couldn't look more dangerous on this otherwise beautiful, calm and peaceful day.

Ready up: Pause

"Ok freeze." Luka narrates. "Power of myths help me, this is so embarrassing. Just for the record, guys, I saw him throwing the rock at me from my peripheral vision, only I was just too preoccupied with the clash happening in my head to react to it. But its not like I want these daydreams to happen when they do. They just, sorta do, ya know? I just wish he understood that sometimes instead of getting on my case about it, but I knew better than to try to explain that to Pop for the one hundredth time, ugh and still, hard as I try I just couldn't keep the words from sneaking off of my tongue and out of my mouth." Luka narrates with a seemingly disappointed tone. "Sorry that's it, I won't butt in again. Okay, okay unfreeze," Luka narrates.

Ready up: Play

"Um, I was just–" Luka begins to say.

"Daydreaming, during your training... Again!" Andrew says in his frustration.

Luka's eyes immediately drops to the floor.

"Yes, I can see that," Andrew says with a tone. "Ugh, what am I going to do with you, Luke, I was only gone for a few minutes. You haven't even worked up a sweat yet." Andrew says.

Luka looks at both of his dry arms.

"What was it this time, huh? What could have possibly been so important that you couldn't have finish your warm-ups before I got back?" Andrew says, as if already knowing the answer.

"Uh... It was the Ar–" Luka starts to say reluctantly.

"Oh! wait, let me guess... it was the Arena Cup Tournament wasn't it... The big act." Andrew says as Luka's anxiety begins to set in. "What was I even thinking when I asked? " Andrew says, slightly sarcastically.

Luka quickly jumps in.

"–But, Dad, it was a really good one this time. It was totally different, I swear," Luka argues noticeably, catching his father's interest.

"Oh? How so?" Andrew says with even more sarcasm.

"Alright, so boom. I was fighting, right? ...I was fighting and you were right. It was the act, the big act, but that wasn't what was most different, it wasn't until after I won that– wait, wait-wait before I say that, I gotta tell you how I won. It was a really good one this time pop for real," Luka says, becoming even more excited by the thought of his own story before actually telling it.

Andrew is immediately filled with frustration.

"Ugh. It's always a good one with you, Luke. Some new special move that you can never seem to pull off in real life, or some new fighting style that never seems to hold up in a real clash," Andrew expresses his frustration. "You know, I didn't move us all the way out here, to the outskirts of Kayuga Territory to train you for some stupid blood sport. How many times must I say it? Fighting for fun isn't the assignment here. There is more to life than simply beating up other people just to say that you can." Andrew sighs. "It sickens me how things are going nowadays...," Andrew says with a seemingly heavy heart.

Luka has already begun to roll his eyes.

"Here we go–" Luka says under his breath.

"It wasn't always like this, ya know. Things were different back in the old day. People were different. People actually shared promise, discipline, and genuine care for their fellow neighbors," Andrew says proudly as he looks off into the sky.

Meanwhile Luka is mouthing his words with his lips while he isn't looking.

"Promise, discipline, and genuine care for our fellow neighbors." Luka mocks. "I know all that already, but come on, Dad, the world is different now. You heard the same stories I have. The world is a lot more exciting now than it was before. Better even!" Luka argues trying to make his case.

"And how would you know, huh? How Luke? How? A story is only as good as the person who tells it. For all you know, it could be just that–a mythical story. Anyone whose anyone can tell one, and it doesn't always mean it's true especially if the person whose telling it is only speaking to get a reaction from you." Andrew sighs. "I just don't get it. What's the big thirst of being some famous fighter or someone chasing clouds anyway?" Andrew says, genuinely confused.

Luka makes a screwed face,

"Chasing clouds? Wait, do you mean someone chasing clout?" Luka responds, even more confused but is then amused.

"Huh?" Andrew says, completely lost now.

"Huh?" Luka repeats mocking him with a tone. "You would sound like such a ol' timer if I knew one," Luka says with a tone jokingly.

Andrew folds his arms in defiance and makes a helpless face.

"What?" Andrew says standing by what he said.

"Hehe, I think you mean clout," says Luka, but Andrew doesn't budge. "You know, clout? It's what 'everyone is chasing.' Come on, Dad, you're not this old. The reputation of Monarch is the highest level of clout there is. Clout is reputation and reputation is currency. Monarchs rule. With that kind of reputation, you can pretty much do anything, go anywhere, publicly destroy your opponents, and have people love you for it. You're like... you're like, fake—the king of all the lands or something, for real," Luka says with promise but Andrew isn't convinced. "Wasn't the world controlled by powerful burgs and armies back in your "old-days"? Back when everyone was clashing and constantly at war with each other. You've been to the burg's for supplies, you've said it yourself, don't you think everyone gets along a lot better nowadays, now that clout is the only goal and not total borough domination? Or are all those stories not true either?" Luka says dominantly.

"I've only ever said people are less on edge in the burgs these days but, that's just it, even back then it wasn't about total control, the Hystalorians got it wrong. Only the south was at war with one another over land, the north didn't participate in that. They only fought to end the suffering of the people. And that, my boy, is my point. We 'Ol Timers' fought for a purpose greater than ourselves back then. We fought for the future. When are you gonna realize that there's more to life than clouts," Andrew says passionately.

"...It's clout, Dad, just clout. No *s*. It's already plural like fruit and most good things." Luka says

"Like Dojakai." Andrew says indifferently.

"Exactly, now say it with me, clout—cl-ow-tuh. I know it's the *T* that gets you. It has to roll off your tongue, Ol Timer, cl-ow-T he he," Luka jokes.

Even Andrew breaks into a light chuckle.

"Clout just makes us better than we were before, and I don't know... maybe I could understand your side and this future you claimed to have fought for if you'd stop telling me what I already know and just tell me, what the assignment is? Or exactly what is the reason we're living on the edge of this cliff! In Kayuga Territory—alone—with no contact no nothing but training equipment and the clothes on our back," Luka says, becoming anxiously frustrated.

"...We have a house," Andrew says sarcastically.

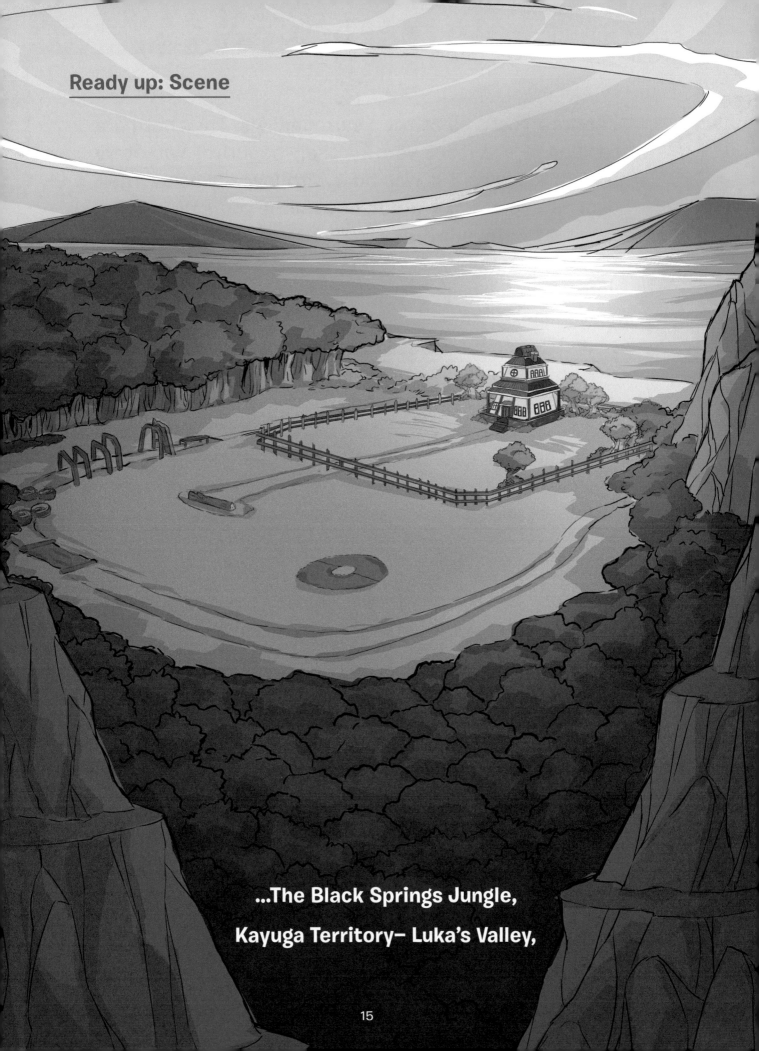

...The Black Springs Jungle,

Kayuga Territory– Luka's Valley,

Andrew gestures at their surroundings. They both are standing in the front yard of their beautiful two-story home. It looks as if it was built with love, by hand. Their house is enclosed by a gorgeous do-it-yourself wooden fence that surrounds them. The house and fence is painted in a way, camouflaged to match the surrounding area. The fence itself separates them from a huge open field that leads to a small forest. There's training equipment set up all over the field. At first glance, you'd see some work-out weights, a combat circle, an obstacle course, a few piles of chopped wood, and large piles of stones stacked strategically all around their yard. Their home sits at the edge of a cliff and below the house is a small beach leading to the open ocean located behind them. The beach, their house, and the surrounding forest are all towered over by several mountains creating a secluded valley. All while being completely surrounded by a huge unforgivable jungle in middle of nowhere.

...Luka is still stewing.

"You know what we're doing out here." Andrew says reassuringly.

"Do I?" Luka asks sarcastically.

"We're training," Andrew says reassuringly.

"So am I learning to clash or nah? Because fighting and training seems a lot like the other, if you ask me. Why not test my skill in front of the world if you really wanna know if it's catching? Why not let me compete? This is so unfair, Mythics!" Luka claims.

"Hey!! Now I've always allowed you to speak your mind freely with me, but don't get carried away after I've put you to sleep!" Andrew warns. "We don't call on the Myths that way in this house, you hear me?!" He says dominantly, Luka's frustration surrenders to his better judgment. "You know what your training is for Luke, and in case you forgot, let me remind you. It's simply for the protection of our purpose. That's it, and before you ask me, the answer as always remains the same. I will tell you that purpose when–," Andrew starts sternly with dominance, completely asserting himself.

"When I'm ready, yeah, I know," Luka says softly. "But see, I'm getting older now and I've sorta been thinking more sensibly ya know. I realized something, I always get stuck on the purpose part, what's the purpose? When is the purpose, why is there a purpose?! Ya know, but lately it's been more of the protection part that I've been worrying about. Why do we need Protection? For what? From who?! No one even knows we exist. You've gotta snap out of it Popsicle, no one's coming!–that PTSD gotchu tripping tripping. The world is at peace ...I think? You know, according to...–whatever, You get my sense. And! You keep saying 'our' purpose and not 'my' purpose, which also has ya boy thinking, if we're talking about us here, you and me, shouldn't I have a say in all of this," Luka rants while Andrew tries to keep up and pay attention. "And I say what purpose could possibly be more important than having the reputation of Monarch?! You sense me or nah?! You always say 'I'll tell you when you're ready,'" Luka says with a tone. "But when? When will I be ready?!" Luka says, really letting his emotions show.

"When you're ready?" Andrew says, closing his eyes and keeping cool.

"Arg! This is foo–" Luka says, losing it.

"Luka, cool it with the slang ok! You're barely even making sense when you talk anymore so no, I don't sense you. Listen, you're my son not one of those kids from Lockaz you seem to love so much. And foo?! . . . what's foo?" Andrew says, also becoming frustrated.

"Foo as in Foo-lish, you know, when–" Luka begins annoyingly.

"I know what foo means. I'm saying, foo? what's foo about this?" Andrew says quickly.

"You! You're foo!" Luka says defiantly.

"Auraluke!" Andrew says, thunderingly clenching his fists.

In that instance there is a huge screeching cry heard from in the distance. Luka immediately regains himself, becoming nervous from the feral cry. There is a slight pause until Luka lowers his caution.

"I bet if Mom were here, she'd tell me why...," Luka mutters under his breath.

"Enough already, mind yourself or you'll excite one of them," Andrew says cautiously.

Luka stays silent but can't seem to let it go as his face remains visibly filled with emotion as his eyebrows twitch. Andrew and Luka sits in silence for a bit longer until finally Andrew first finishes working through his own emotions only to realize Luka is still upset. Andrew realizes the seriousness of their situation and inhales a deep breath of fresh air. Andrew tries to lighten himself up to a more pleasant tone of expression. Rubbing the back of his neck, he begins to smirk a bit.

"So, you gonna tell me what was so different about your daydreams this time, or is that foo too? Who was the opponent?" Andrew says as nonchalantly as he possibly could without allowing his voice or body language to seem affected by their last exchange of words.

Just then an unknown figure runs swiftly through the jungle toward their house. His feet are moving fast as he runs and jumps over what seems to be naturally fallen tree barks, strategically placed in a way to block the path to their house.

"What was so different about what, bro?" Luka says as if he has already forgotten why he was upset.

The unknown man is running faster. Now you can see there is a rope strapped to his leg, as well as his dark red-and-diamond-plated metal sash.

"One, I'm not your bro, and two, you know what," Andrew says, realizing Luka is completely lost. "I'm talking about the punching bag," Andrew says as Luka begins to stare off slightly. Andrew looks at Luka with a broken heart expression but lightens up even more. "You know the guy, the one you always seem to put the beats on in those daydreams of yours?" Andrew says with more enthusiasm.

"Oh! He he, yea I don't know what you're talking about haha," Luka laughs with a coy smirk.

"Oh, you know exactly what I'm talking about. It was me again, wasn't it? Wasn't it?!" Andrew says jokingly.

Luka bursts into laughter as his distant gaze flashes back to the tournament from his imagination.

Ready up: Flashback

… Inside Luka's imagination,

Suddenly Luka is flying through mid air spinning, Andrew gets dropkicked in the face with crazy impact by Luka and is knocked unconscious immediately.

"Oh, he cracked him! He cracked him! That's it! That's it!" the speculator screams with excitement.

Andrew can been seen on the floor, all beaten up.

Ready Up: Scene

Back to reality, Andrew and Luka are both laughing now.

"I'm just saying, in all actuality that move would never land so perfectly in a real clash." Andrew says.

"What?! I could totally land that move in real life" Luka argues.

"Your imagination really is something though, tell you what, maybe if I won at least once in your dreams, I'd be inclined to take these moves a little more seriously. Somehow in your dreams, I'm always losing, or getting beaten to a pulp. Then I have to listen to you tell this epic story about how I get folded," Andrew says, genuinely entertained.

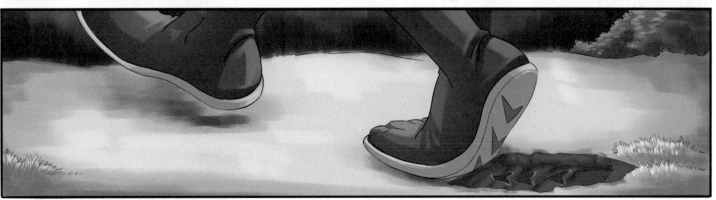

Actually, I don't even remember our fight that clearly.

After I packed you up, something else happened.

I was just about to be crowned Dojakai Monarch Champion when all of a sudden, out of nowhere... Hm?

21

The unknown person is running even faster toward their house, his forearm and shoulder armor glaring and gleaming every time it manages to catch the sun from within the shade of the thick jungle above.

"Actually, I don't even remember our fight that clearly. After I packed you up, something else happened . . . I was just about to be crowned Dojakai Monarch Champion when all of a sudden, out of nowhere... Hm?" Luka begins.

Luka pauses mid sentence and anxiously looks up past the fence of his front yard, through the open field and toward the tree line at the start of the forest.

"Did you hear that?" Luka says, turning to Andrew who is already looking in the direction of the intruder.

"Something is coming. It could be anything. Ready up!" Andrew says seriously.

Luka tries to prepare for a coming attack but finds himself no longer in control of his own body as he slowly begins to step back in a slowly retreat until finally he backs into his father. Andrew looks down at him noticing his fear and steps in front of him, standing firm and protective.

Pressure!

"**O**kay freeze, I know I said I wouldn't butt in again, but I just can't help it. I don't know what it is but there's just something about my life that doesn't feel normal. Dad's always talking about purpose and what I still need to learn to understand that purpose, but he never actually tells me what the purpose is. It's like he's just messing with me on purpose, ya know know what I mean. Did you see how I almost got him with the whole 'well what are we protecting' thing? And he still flipped it Ugh, it's so annoying how he does that. It probably doesn't help that whenever we start talking about it, things just start to go left. We both have this thing with our emotions that when lit just seems to spiral pretty quickly. I never seem to notice when it happens to me, but Dad seems to have a better handle on it. I know he doesn't mean it, and I think he knows I don't mean it either. I just think its been pretty tough growing up, with no woman of the house, and I know being a single parent can't be easy on the old guy. We both are just so alone–him without his wife and me without, a mom. Sometimes I forget we are all we have in this world. It's just us at the top of this cliff we call home, so that means we have to look out for each other, protect one another. Wait, is that it? Is that the purpose we're protecting? Us? Was it always about 'us' and our little family? I think I get it now. We have to protect this life of ours because there's no one else that will. Everyone else is only worried about their own lives, especially in the big city and if anything ever happens, to either of us in this family it would leave the others all alone, like how Pop and I are now and if that happened, then where would that leave our family? It would make sense why he trains me so hard. It may not seem like it at times but he knows things about this world that I didn't. It's just I would hear stories about how cool life can be in the big city and it makes me regret being here, with him, away from all the action. Truthfully, I don't even know why I'm so obsessed with tournaments, it just sucks feeling like you don't exist, like no one cares, because you're cloutless. I know it bugs Dad, but when I'm in my mode, I kinda want it to ya know. He never holds it against me though. He always helps to keep me focused on what's most important and that's family. My dad's always, protecting me from stuff—even from things I don't know I need protection from, like my own childish emotions... Speaking of childish emotions, please don't judge me for what happens next, okay? I could sense the shift in the air, something was coming. I didn't know if it was a Dojakai, stranger, or dad's worse fear coming true. All I knew was that this was definitely not happening within the safety of my temples, this was real. I was under a lot of pressure," Luka narrates.

Pressure!: Scene

   ...Back to Luka's house,

25

Luka is standing close by Andrew, looking to him as his anxiety continues to grows at the thought of the approaching clash. Finally a man comes diving out of the forest into the open field in front of the yard. He stops right at the tree line holding his position. He looks around for a bit, scanning the entire area. His eyes wander, with acute purpose, nearly spotting Luka standing behind Andrew. Just then the man notices Andrew, nearly seeing him too. He becomes even more nervous at the man's deadly glare. The man is in a BrixCity Academy uniform—a skintight protective bodysuit that covers him from neck to toe with dark red gloves. However, he is also wearing dark-red armor with platinum trims on his shoulders, forearms, and hips. There is an amulet on his chest attached to a fish scale chain wrapped over his shoulder and under his arm which goes around his upper body. His armor and jewelry dances with the sunlight brightly as he steps out from the shade of the trees and into the open. Luka is frozen in shock and is in a state of awe by the man's presence. He quickly flashes back to his daydream and sees the same man standing in the same pose, only with less armor. Luka comes back to reality still staring at the man in disbelief.

"It can't be, it... It's actually him?" Luka says.

Luka leans over to see if Andrew is as surprised to see the man as he is, but he is just glaring at the man intensely as if he is prepared for anything to happen, including a clash of wills.

"Focus, Auraluke!" Andrew says promptly. "Who knows why he's here?" Andrew says sternly.

What are you doing here?!

Dad?!

27

Luka looks back towards the man while still leaning out from behind Andrew. The man still scanning the area finally spots Luka hiding behind Andrew. Without any prompts or incentives, he immediately bursts into an all out sprint toward their house with so much vigor that his first few steps literally digs into the ground, blasting dirt back beneath his feet. The man is flying towards them, jumping, flipping, and hurdling, parkouring over all obstacles standing in his way. He flips over their tractor, diving over other training equipment swiftly and with style. Luka becomes even more uneasy as the man quickly makes it through the field and straight to their front yard. He dives over their fence, finally breaking his stride landing and begins walking straight up to them. Andrew makes a protective stance in front of Luka who looks back and forth between his father and the man. Without a single word being spoken, the man walks right up to Andrew and throws a straight punch. Andrew grabs his fist out mid air and quickly spins him around twisting his arm behind his back.

"What are you doing here?!" Andrew asks aggressively.

"Dad?" Luka asks anxiously.

The man looks over his shoulder at Luka and releases a dark smirk. Luka becomes even more nervous.

"Dad?!" Luka asks even more anxiously.

Luka slowly begins to pace a few steps back toward their house preparing for the worse. Andrew briefly glances back in concern of Luka, and in that instant, the man flips out of Andrew's hold, simultaneously kicking him in the chest, rolling then flipping up to his feet some distance away from Andrew. The man immediately begins to run at Luka again, but Andrew steps in front of his path, extending one hand, showing that he cannot pass him. The man smiles again then reaches behind him for his armored waist belt and grabs a small cylinder with a speared tip. He pushes a button, and the cylinder opens, extending into a staff like spear in an instant. The speared tip is made up of three shards. The biggest shard sits on top while the other two connected are underneath, all forming a pointed tip. The sun shines bright, glaring off the tip of the lead shard. Luka is stunned with amazement. Andrew's eyebrows only twitch once as he stays locked on the man's next movement. The man aims the staff over his arm, resting the tip of the spear on his elbow aiming at Luka. He pushes a button on the small golden remote built into the center of the staff. The top shard suddenly blasts out from the staff at great speed past Andrew's waist, striking the dirt behind him by Luka's feet.

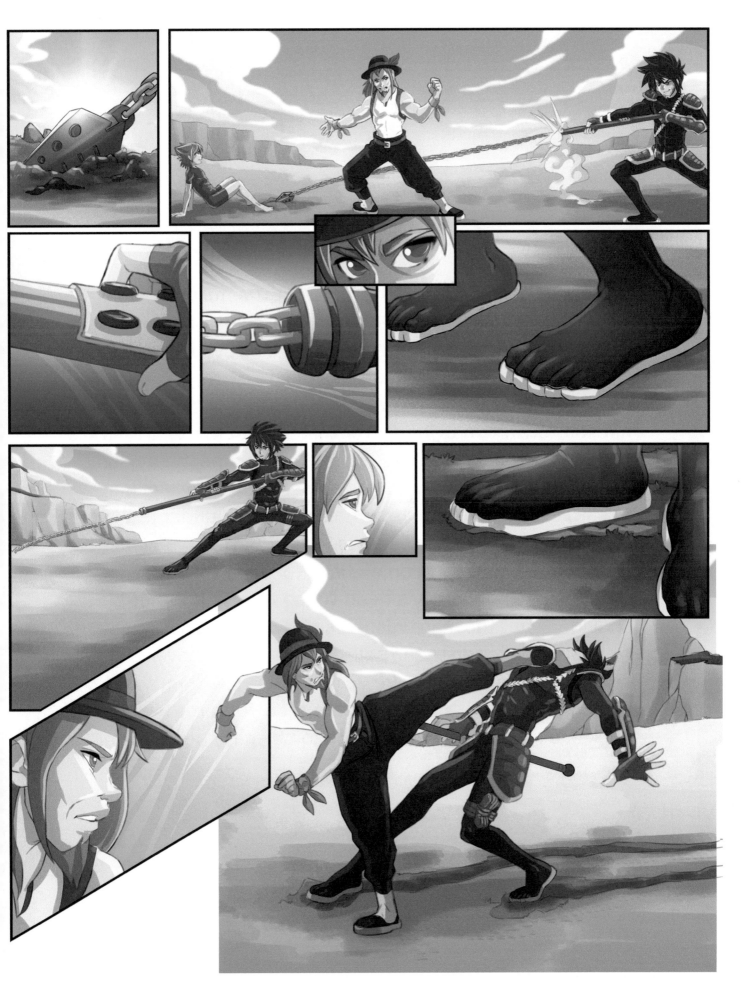

The shard is attached to a seemingly never-ending chain which connects to the inside of the hollowed pole. The man begins running at Andrew, then pushes the button again. The chain tightens and so does his grip on the pole. It immediately snatches him forward, retracting at incredible speeds so fast that he begins to zip-line himself forward, moving faster than he would have trying to run at them. Replanting his feet as he zips, he begins sliding at them now, it begins to seem as if he's gliding toward them. His feet has a protective layer under it. Dirt kicks back behind him. Andrew waits patiently for him to approach, and as soon as he is in range, he throws a round-house at the guy's head trying to kick it off of his shoulders, but the man twists his body, leaning backward, while still holding on to the pole dodging it. He weaves back smoothly underneath Andrew's powerful kick, then stops, turns around and thrusts his armored forearm into his back causing him to stumble off somewhere behind him.

The man finally retracts the shard and chain by Luka's feet, finding himself not far from Luka, now between them both. Luka slowly puts up his fists, but by his slight trembles, it is clear he isn't actually prepared to fight. Luka's anxiety grows as the man stares him down, his face becoming even more uncertain. The man can't help but release a calm smirk.

"C'mon kid, really?" the man says with a slightly rough tone.

His face looks as if surprised that Luka would even attempt to fight. In that instant, Andrew instantly slides in front of the man view, holding his arm out protectively once again, this time surprising him.

"No, really!" Andrew says.

He clenches his fist so tight that his veins burst out of his muscles. He cocks back a punch, swinging with the intention of breaking something.

"Ah!" Andrew blurts.

Andrew throws the punch with tremendous power at the man. Andrew's fist connects banging into the man's chin with so much force that the man's head jerks back. He almost stumbles back but firmly stands on his back leg to catch himself. There is a pause between them as Luka looks on. After a second Andrew suddenly expresses pain in his face, while the man wears a proud smirk. Andrew grunts a bit as he lowers his fist a bit to reveal his punch connected with the metal faceplate that the man is wearing. He had waited until the very last second to raise his chin into it punch purposely. The man's smirk quickly becomes an intense frown as he then swiftly ducks under Andrew's fist, spins around, and elbows him in his stomach with a powerful blow of his own. Andrew feels that one, then the man spins around again now rolling his weapon around his neck and over his head, twisting and smacks Andrew in the face with the flat side of the metal shard tip.

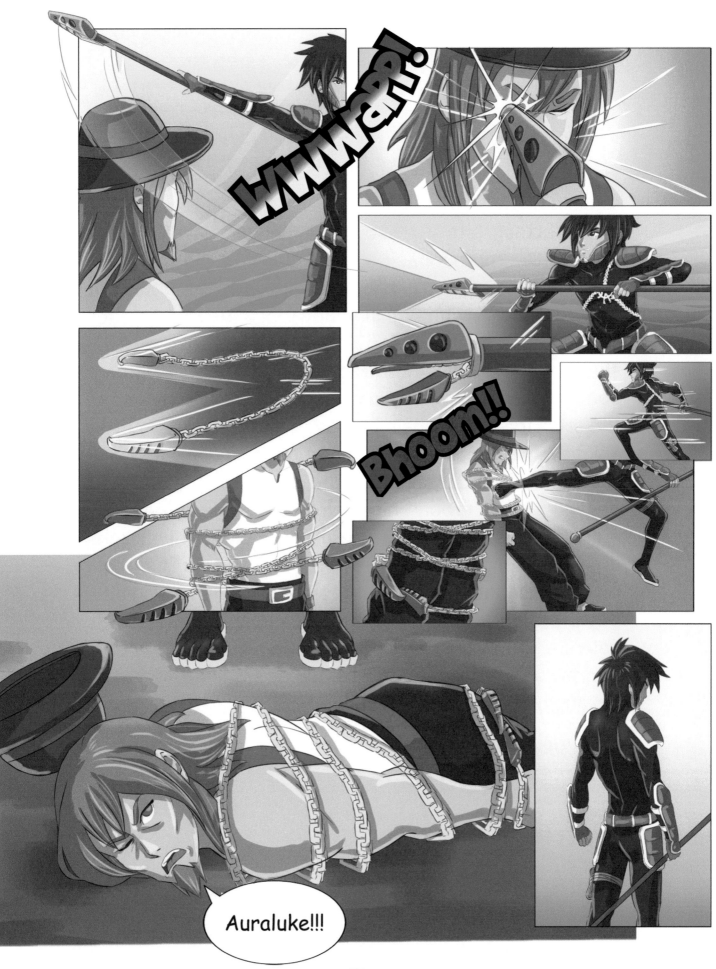

The attack hits with so much power that it causes Andrew to stumble back again. This time the man flips the staff over, first aiming at Luka, but then turns it toward Andrew, who is just recovering. The man pushes two buttons on the weapon and shoots both bottom shards blast out at Andrew instead. The two shards are connected by a single chain which is no longer attached to the stick itself. The chain and two shards fly out, Andrew unknowingly turns around just in time as the middle of the double shard's chain hit the center of his chest. It begins to wrap around his entire body, quickly tying his arms down at his sides. The man simultaneously runs up and jumps, kicking Andrew in the chest as the chain magnetically locks around his legs, causing him to stumble back. Andrew is trapped. He hops a bit, trying to keep his balance before eventually falling face first into the dirt. Andrew squirms on the floor as he struggles to get free, looking back at Luka with concern.

"Auraluke!" Andrew calls fearfully.

Luka is backing up now, even more nervous. The strange man turns to Luka then looks down at his weapon and then back at Luka once more. He pushes a button shrinking the spear back to its small cylinder form and tosses it into the air. He takes off toward Luka. While he is running, the cylinder falls near his waist belt and is magnetically caught immediately latches itself onto his hip. The man sprinting gets closer and closer to his target Luka, pulling back his fist, preparing to strike.

"Ah!" He screams out in rage.

He leans in to strike when finally Luka breaks his guard and curls up in a ball, shutting his eyes, guarding his face and screams in a high pitched tone.

"Ahhh! Okay! Okay! Uncle Eiko! Stop! I give up! You got this one!" Luka says panicking.

Luka assumes the worse, but nothing happened. There is a awkward pause of silence for a second, until finally he becomes slightly confused that he hasn't been hit yet. He slowly peaks through the opening in his guard and sees Eiko's fist is holding just inches from connecting with his face.

"Yeah, that's what I thought, you little 'BeFa', ha ha. Long time no see, nephew, Hey look ...no pressure!," Eiko says teasingly.

Eiko opens his fist and waves at Luka. Luka allows himself to let his guard down and allows himself to lighten up instantly.

"Haha Chop!" Eiko calls.

"Oh No!" Luka says realizing what he'd just done.

Over Luka's head is Eiko's other hand, but it's too late for Luka to react. He immediately hammers the side of his hand into the back of Luka's neck, so forcefully Luka nearly goes unconscious but Eiko quickly snatching him up under his arm in a headlock, jamming his knuckle into Luka's head, ruffling his hair around a bit finally slapping him in the back of the head. Luka, in distress, begins to laugh.

"Combo no back-sies head-wop, We always accept our challenges..." Eiko says playfully.

Luka slightly embarrassed by his own fear to clash with his uncle, accepts his punishment gracefully.

"Wow, check out this hair it's touching your shoulders, and these cuts, you're ripped now... You've really rushed up since the last time I've seen you, huh lil bro," Eiko says proudly.

Andrew clears his throat from in the distance. Eiko and Luka both look over their shoulders at him. He is still tied up on the floor. Luka giggles childishly, but Andrew gives him a serious look from over on his stomach, and he immediately stops. Luka can't help but be amused by his father's defeat to his uncle and hero, Eiko.

Nothing Over Family

...Luka's House,

Eiko walks over to Andrew and releases him from the double shard-an-chain then helps him up. Eiko finds the center of the chain marked by a single gold metal link and puts it underneath the lead shard on a hook, which grabs the double shard's chain, and retracts them back into their original places.

"Thanks," Andrew says standing to his feet, he breaths in a huge sigh of relief with a deep stretch. "Whew! Either I'm getting old or you've really rushed up since your last visit yourself there little brother. You've gotten a lot stronger. Heh, It's funny just when I think you're at your best, you' push past your limits an get even better. Myths will us the academy has really done a great job molding you," Andrew says proudly.

Andrew then rubs his hand and shakes off the pain from punching Eiko's metal face plate.

"Sorry about that, Andrew, I know it's long overdue but you told me not to go easy on you two my next visit out. You said Auraluke needed a more realistic combat situation," Eiko says.

"Absolutely, and I meant every word of it. Which also makes me ask you, why did you stop attacking?" Andrew asks.

"Oh, Well, because Auraluke stopped defending, he had no will to fight the clash was won," Eiko says justifiably.

"What's with credentials, bro," Luka says under his breath, trying to seem unamused.

"But that's just it," Andrew butts in. "In a realistic combat situation, an enemy wouldn't stop attacking just because 'Luka' stopped defending. He needs to understand the difference between his 'training' and the real thing. I'm afraid he lacks the focus and courage needed to engage his enemy in a real clash," Andrew says with a disappointing sigh. "I suppose that one's on me, but this is why he needs to experience more of the real thing, so he understands the seriousness of a clashing of wills. So yeah, do me a favor will ya? Next time, don't stop," Andrew says, turning to Luka intensely.

Eiko looks back at Luka, who is noticeably hurt by Andrew's tone.

"Ya know, sometimes I feel the same way. Sometimes I doubt myself too," Eiko says encouragingly. "The trick is to find the purpose for the action—your reason for fighting to begin with. Only, it has to be a something or someone you actually feel really strongly about, and then you draw strength from that feeling. I'm always afraid to fight. I use this technique a lot," Eiko says unashamed.

"You, Eiko? Afraid to fight? Are you kidding? You're an empire, you're untouchable, unmatched, unbeatable! Maybe even stronger than Dad," Luka says passionately.

Andrew begins to clear his throat.

"Hold on Pop-alot, I'ma let you finish... but for-real just look at you Unc, strong, fast, and stylish! C'mon, what more do they want, just look at the physique, talk about ripped, not to mention, the gear," Luka says with superb admiration. "And this?! Just what in the he** is this thing?" Luka says in complete awe, peeking around at Eiko's weapon, still on his hip.

"Hey! Language! I swear your uncle Eiko shows up, and all of a sudden, you start talking like an academy kid," Andrew says.

"Chill, Papa-Don. This is how I always talk, bro," Luka says obliviously.

"I'm not your . . ., " Andrew starts to say but gives up half way with a helpless sigh. "What's the point anymore?" Andrew says helplessly.

He shakes his head and rubs his temples. Luka smiles proudly at his fathers mental defeat as he proceeds to grab Eiko's weapon off of his hip, pushing several buttons instinctively. The staff suddenly pops open into a staff at the same time shooting the lead shard and chain out past Andrew's face, slamming into the house some distance away. Luka is stunned. Completely oblivious to nearly taking Andrew out, too distracted by Eiko's new gear to notice as he continues to examines the staff.

"Be careful, Auraluke. It's kinda sensitive lil-bro," Eiko says sharing a look with Andrew.

"What is it? How does it work, bro-bro?" Luka says, completely unable to hold back his excitement now.

"It's kinda hard to explain if you've never studied IV Engineering at an academy. But it's called an AD-Stick or a Pop-Rod if your hip, you sense me, all AD's need one to be sanctioned."

"I sense you bro, I'm so sensitized right now it's not even funny, wait no that didn't come out right" Luka says trying to gauge his uncles cool meter.

"Right... Anyway, like I was saying all AD's need one, mine is pretty special to me. I designed all the alterations myself. It's completely tailored to my anatomy, from its height, to weight and its functionality. It's all me in there through and through. I even tricked out the sensitivity scale on the controller. Its even been modified to match the strength and grip in each of my fingers," Eiko can't help to explain proudly.

"Awesome! Did you always have it? Why is this my first time seeing it? C'mon, man, why is you holding out, what's the juice?" Luka says obsessively.

"Myths help us," Andrew says, walking away towards the house to remove the shard.

"I didn't? That's weird, hm." Eiko shrugs. "Maybe it was in the shop." Eiko says

Andrew glances back but then continues towards the house.

"As a promising AD, in the academy acquiring an AD-Stick is the only thing anyone can ever cares about. It's the way of life. At first they make you train with an old Sur-Rod. You aren't even allowed to touch a custom AD-Stick until after you've qualify for the sanction," Eiko explains.

"Sanction?" Andrew asks, returning with the tip of the shard.

"I know how it sounds, but it's actually a great honor. See in the old times AD's weren't among the hippest of the classes and by many standards still isn't." Eiko says heavily

"What do you mean?" Luka asks genuinely.

"We don't talk about it... it's more like an, if you know, you know sorta thing. Its just back then, it was considered a title of banishment, a fool's errand even, used more as a punishment than an honorable achievement. You was alive back then right? You remember how it was, Andrew," Eiko says.

"I'm afraid I was just a boy back then. Besides my people lived outside of the tribes of men in the old times. But that's interesting, considering a sanction an honor," Andrew says.

"Being sanctioned as an AD is the only way you get to compete in cups and represent your banner. It's actually one of the hardest accolades in the academy to acquire. I've been sanctioned for a little over three years now. A lot of the kids drop out in the first year of the AD brackets. It's not for everybody," Eiko claims.

"An AD, huh? Oh! Wait I remember that one. You said that it stands for something, right? Something weird . . . I just had it. It was... Oh right. It meant advanced diving, right?! Like, to be a Diver, sorta how you dive over stuff all fancy like ya know, shhew! Weee! Ya know," Luka says, jumping his hand acrobatically off itself through the air.

"It means Adverse Dynamics, as in to be Adversely Dynamic," Eiko says, completely unamused.

"Ah, I was kinda close." Luka shrugs confidently.

"Right, kinda," Eiko says, shaking his head bewildered. "Hehe, Adverse Dynamics teaches us the art of remaining in control of your mind, body, and range of motion no matter how impossible an obstacles standing in front of you may seem and, still managing to come out of the situation successfully," Eiko says seriously. "But I always liked the term coined by the Great AD Kaimen, first of his name, before the crowning of the first monarchs. He simply saw himself as an Adventurist," Eiko explains with a sense of hope lingering. "But he, unfortunately, was the first and the last to ever really do it," Eiko closes.

"That's the guy that made the first pilgrimage, right? The one that found the Dojakai?" Luka says eagerly.

"Do you want me to speak about the way of the AD, or are you going to keep interrupting?" Eiko says, becoming slightly frustrated.

"I'm sorry. I do, it's just that Dad doesn't know any of this good stuff, so I have to ask you everything I need to know while I gotchu here, Uncle Eiko. You sense me right?," Luka says innocently.

Andrew makes a face clinching his lips. He and Eiko share a look. Andrew then shakes his head. Eiko answers while still locking eyes with Andrew.

"Sure, Neph, I sense you," Eiko says with a tone turning back to Luka. "But it wasn't just him. The Great AD Kaimen, first of his name, on the pilgrimage, I mean. It was also the father of the Dojakai and creator of the first Sur-Rod who made the trip. They discovered the Dojakai together, at a time where mankind and all of our class systems were out of ideas on how to survive the growingly harsh environments that plagued us. Lore facts has it that their plunge into the unknown was pre-documented in the oldest book of the oldest tome in time. They called their journey the Great AD Venture, which yes led to the discovery of Dojakai, the M-Pocs, and essentially the beginning of the new world," Eiko says ominously, holding a slight pause. "But getting back on the topic of AD-Sticks. . .," Eiko says, changing back to his original tone, "I'd say it happens around year three of the AD Brackets. The BrixCity Academy just hands you a stump of cedar oak, and . . .," Eiko starts.

"Cedars! We have cedar trees with Cedar Oak, look!" Luka says, pointing proudly to the nearby trees in their front yard.

"Nah, those look like the hybrid knockoffs of the real thing. Prolly got them from the Five Blox section in the 'City of Brix Territory'. The real ones—real cedars—are ten times as big, huge, and can only survive near active volcanoes. Cedar oak is a special kind of wood because it's the only one with metal properties to it. They've always existed in Penyow, but their flowers never bloomed until the Dojakai came, according to the lore facts. Some say it's the strongest property known to man, others say it's the source of BrixCity's strength. The stump that the academy gives to us makes you feel as if you've been carrying around a ton of bricks around all day, and your professors must see you with it by your side at all times or risk being kicked out of the bracket. We're forced to tote it around like an accessory for six months until finally you're allowed to use it to carve out your very own custom AD-Stick." Eiko says casually.

"Nice," Luka says glancing over to an old log in their front yard.

"From there, you are granted one additional alteration for every challenge accepted and won, against an opposing school . . . I don't know, incentives to win, I guess," Eiko shrugs.

Luka admires how many buttons and alterations Eiko's AD-Stick has and is amazed by him.

"{Eiko is so cool. I can't believe we're actually related..}" Luka thinks to himself, too embarrassed to say it out loud.

Luka stares at him with a creepy face. Eiko gets a bit creeped out a bit but pretends he isn't.

"The school then provides you access to the Architechs, and based on your understandings of physics from IV-Engineering 20.10 and your take on surviving the elements from Trench-Talk 20.51, the Architechs will basically build you the perfect tool for survival. The Architechs can pretty much build anything that physics allows, but as you know, the influence of Dojakai and their manipulation over the elements has obviously completely changed what we knew to be physically possible," Eiko explains.

"Obviously," Luka says confidently.

Andrew shakes his head again, this time nearly passing out in his annoyance.

"You good, Paparazzi? Go get you some water or sum," Luka says carelessly. "I'm sorry, Unc. He still thinks clout is short for forecasts, say nothing, I know you sense me . . . Continue," Luka says confidently.

Eiko smirks to himself.

"Anyway, my AD-Stick is still not finished yet. I still have a few ideas in mind for the final design. It's a pretty long process building them from scratch, but when they're finished, your AD-Stick is less of a tool for survival and more sorta like a best friend. We've been through a lot together me my ol' Pop-Rod," Eiko explains.

"Whoa, I mean cool! An actual best friend, huh? Amazing . . . So does everyone in the academy get one?" Luka says obliviously.

"Did you hear anything?! I literally just . . ." Eiko sighs quickly glancing at Andrew. "No, only students with an AD classification on their third year can even begin to think about having one. And only those who are sanctioned are allowed to see the Architechs. Not to mention how hard it is to even last with a Cedar Stump in the Bracket. Everyone else has to wait until they've already graduated or would have to try an join an already sanctioned crew to get one, and even then there's a huge waiting list to see the Architect if you don't have any clout," Eiko says.

"See," Luka says confidently in Andrew's direction.

"You have no idea how hard I had to work to earn this, nephew," Eiko says ominously.

Luka quickly dazes off slipping into a little daydream imagining countless enemies falling at Eiko's feet, but forcefully snaps himself out of it.

"Well, if I went to BrixCity Academy, I'd get one in three months tops, ha ha ha! You sense me right Dad," Luka claims.

Andrew sips from a cup staring off into space.

"Yeah . . . right—Hey, Andrew, you know it isn't too late for Auraluke to register for the BCA next semester. I think he could really learn a lot from attending the academy," Eiko says with a tone only Andrew would notice.

Andrew nearly choked on his water, looking as if doesn't look like he likes that idea.

"I'm only saying, with the training he already has from you, I bet he could really benefit from some of the organized activities BCA has to offer. Besides, it's very safe," Eiko says, still in tone.

Luka looks back and forth between them and begins to smile at the idea of him going to school. Andrew begins to lighten up a bit, putting on his best persona.

"I don't know about that one, Eiko. Wouldn't that be a little unfair for the other kids? Luke's pretty strong for his age, and besides that, you know he doesn't have any official papers. He'll never pass the BCC's Credential Legacy Agreement," Andrew says, ending the tone.

Andrew gestures to their surroundings.

"I don't know, I mean, isn't there ways around that sorta thing? I mean, I got in, didn't I?" Eiko argues.

"Your case was a little different, little brother. Your credentials were only destroyed, but the BrixCity Council and DKD keeps their own credential records of all legacies born in their occupied burgs, originally born in the burgs or otherwise. I only needed to alter your papers a bit to avoid questions," Andrew talks back. "Tell you what, let's talk about it over dinner. You're staying, right?" Andrew asks.

Eiko looks back toward the forest where he came from with a concerned expression, then back at Andrew unsatisfied.

"Is something wrong, Eiko? It's been so long. No way you could come all the way out here just to leave so soon. You're not gonna make me beg, are you?" Andrew pleads.

Eiko lowers his head with his ears heightened directly toward the forest from which he came then back up at Andrew, raising his head and smiling pleasantly.

"Of course not bro, of course not," Eiko says, more sure the second time. "It's actually been a while since I've had a home-cooked meal," Eiko says.

"Yes! Two years in the making, to be exact," Luka says ecstatic.

They begin to walk to the house.

"Hope you like coco bread and crab cakes. Should be the catch of the day," Andrew says proudly. "Hey, Luke, why don't you tell your uncle about your daydream from earlier today. I'm sure he'd love to hear it," Andrew says sarcastically.

"Oh, hehe . . . like, right now? Uh, how about we let Eiko tell some stories about what's been going on with him instead. I wanna know more about what's been going on in BrixCity. Besides, Eiko doesn't care about my stupid space-outs, right, Uncle Eiko?" Luka says with a little embarrassment.

"No, that's enough about BrixCity for one day, and what are you talking about, son? Your stories are legendary. Come on, somebody else has to hear this. I can't be the only one so lucky to hear them. Eiko, you wanna hear about his daydreams, right? Luka tells one once a night. It's like a family tradition at this point," Andrew says even convincingly.

Eiko is confused as they all leave from out of the front yard and into the house.

"Eiko?" Luka says hopeful.

"Something more important on your mind little brother?" Andrew stops to ask.

"Important? No, there's nothing over family. Who am I to break tradition. Only it better make more sense than the last one I heard, cause... bro." Eiko says, slightly amused to himself.

Everyone begins to burst out in laughter as they walk in. After a short time the sun slowly begins to set on their home and little slice of heaven 'in the middle of nowhere' at the edge of the Kayuga jungle.

Raised Ruff

...Lockaz Territory, BrixCity – Tye's house

Ping!

Ping!

Ping!

The sun is setting. There is a loud pinging sound radiating throughout a small neighborhood in Lockaz. It's the sound of metal repeatedly clashing with metal. Lockaz is a gritty-looking place. Dangerous looking even. Most of the homes in the neighborhood are run-down or falling apart. There are huge volcanoes in the distance with a small forest below them, huge Cedar trees are growing closest to the volcanoes. There is farmland on the edge of town by a small river with a few commercial buildings closest to the residential areas. Tye's house is in the better part of town, but the lot of Lockaz is just slums and dirt with barely a concrete pavement to walk on.

Finally we reach Tye's house. As group of teens, all in BrixCity uniforms, runs past his house. They seem to be having a good time, laughing and playing despite their depressing environment. We find Tye in his BrixCity Academy uniform with more armor on his person than the teens playing in the streets. He is in his backyard with high walls separating his home from others. His house has one of the only backyards like this. He is the one kicking the metal pole, that is coming up out of the ground. His shin guard bangs into the pole repeatedly, which is what is making the loud chimes radiating throughout the neighborhood. Each clank seemingly more aggressive than the last, leaving tiny dents in the metal pole itself. His spiky white hair flows down his back.

"{They think they can play with me like this! Play with my legacy. I am the son of Tyler Ruff, a mythodamn hero. Stupid NO-Legs. They've never respected me! They've never respected us or anything about our city! Or it's history! They're all idiots! They don't have any understanding of purpose, legacy, or discipline. They don't have no care for their own neighborhood. Everyone just turned a blind eye, while the NO-Legs damn near turns the whole school against me . . . Me! Like I was a mythodamned Hissee, but I don't need 'em. Why do I even care? Glorifying themselves as BeHa's, Brick-Heads! of all the lies. If my father were here to see this, he'd discipline them all . . . Arg! But I'll be great, I'll remind them who we are. I'll remind them of our legacy—my father's legacy. I swear it, on my mother. I will show them who we are, Father. I'll show them that Brick-Heads we are not...}" Tye thinks to himself.

Tye is livid in his head as he begins to kick the metal pole harder and harder until finally he is interrupted.

"–Honey! It's time to come in now. It's time for dinner. You're working way too hard, my baby. Isn't it the last day of school in a couple of months? Come now, it's the final quarter of the semester. You're the youngest student to be sanctioned in BrixCity's history. Whatever it is you're trying to prove, I'm sure you've proven it tenfold by now," Areeka says, stepping into the doorway that leads into the backyard where Tye is. "I'm so proud of you. If only your father were still here to see how you've turned out. I'm sure he'd be just as proud, more proud even, that's a fact . . . You're so much like him, it's scary," Areeka says staring off at him.

Tye listens but continues to kick the pole. Areeka turns to her girlfriend.

"He's so driven, my baby boy. Sometimes I wish he was more of a slouch just so I could mess with him a bit, ya know. How do you even parent a kid as disciplined as him? I just don't know. Sometimes I'm the one who feels like the bad influence," Areeka jokes with her girlfriend, who laughs along. "My son! It'll be the Summer Chalices in a few months. The academy will be closed. You will be officially sanctioned, don't you think you should be out there with the other kids enjoying yourself, not killing yourself training with your Dad's ol' shin breaker station. You'll never break it in, ya know, I think that's the point. I've watched your father kick that thing over a million times. You work too hard. Don't you think you've earned just a little bit of a break?" Areeka calls to Tye. "I honestly don't know what to say. He doesn't even talk to me anymore." Areeka says to her friend. "Honey?! Okay, fine you keep working hard, your dinner is here when you're ready. I just wanted you to know that I love you and whatever's going on at the academy I'm sure will all get sorted out at the A.C.T's . . . hmm? I'll be rooting for you," Areeka says encouragingly.

"Okay, Ma! I'll come-in in a bit," Tye says sternly.

"Oh! Okay!" Areeka says, somewhat satisfied making a face at her girlfriend.

"Yeah, I'll sort 'em out at the Arena Cup Tournament too," Tye says to himself. "Only I don't plan on waiting that long to eat my food. If it's beef they want then I'll be ready to serve 'em. They will learn to respect our family name, regardless of who they think they are. They think they're so tough, but I was raised Ruff," Tye says to himself. "{Deep sleeps, to all NO-Legs! . . .,}" Tye thinks. "Especially the Double L's, Ah!" Tye screams out.

Tye kicks the metal pole three more times with so much force it causes the pole to dent in, then he changes his pivot flexing his other leg a bit. He kicks the other side of the pole nearly bending the pole into an obtuse shape.

HomeSchooled?

...Kayuga Territory, Luka's house – Inside the house

The sun has set. Laughter comes from inside of the house. It's dark out. Luka is acting out his words at the dinner table.

"No, I'm serious, and then I pounded your face in with my elbow. It was completely epic," Luka says with his elbow in hand.

Everyone is laughing instead of Eiko.

"Amazing, Auraluke. That really is some imagination you got there. But the truth is, you really don't know the first thing about an Arena Cup Tournament competition besides what I tell you, do you?" Eiko says calmly.

Luka becomes a bit serious and slightly embarrassed.

"Yes, I do! I know you must be the last man standing to win the clash, right? Right?" Luka says unsure.

Eiko isn't convinced but gestures for him to continue. Luka looks at Andrew who also gestures him to continue. Luka looks back and forth between Andrew and Eiko before finally dropping his head in defeat.

"Ugh . . . Okay, fine, But I'm literally dying out here with Dad kinfo . . .," Luka says casually.

Andrew is taken back by Luka's slang. He mouths "Kinfo?" to Eiko, pointing to him as if to say, Did he get that one from you? Eiko immediately shakes his head in denouncement. Luka just rambles on obliviously.

"–While I'm just here with no one here to talk to and then there's Popcorn here, his time is pretty much up. And he don't know nothing about Arena Cup Tournaments neither, so I don't know why he's looking at me like I'm the crazy one, and you've been MIA for two whole years too long bro. And, I have literally been dreaming about Arena Cup Tournaments nonstop ever since you told me they exist. So please! You gotta give me something . . . I'm so tired of having the same lonely 'ol daydreams," Luka says frantically exhausted, Eiko pauses.

"Hmm, I sense you. Well, I'm not sure if this would help, but for starters, I only meant you and I will most likely never meet in the same competition at the tournament. So,There is no way we'd ever face off in the ACT as opponents. That right there should eliminate me from your daydreams," Eiko says calmly, while Luka loses his cool which he didn't have much of to begin with.

"Whut! But why?! I need you as a special guest opponent. I've only ever met you and Dad. All of my other opponents are just faceless dummies and trees! I need real life opponents,"

"I'm sorry Auraluke but it just doesn't work that way," Eiko says humorously to himself.

"No, I'll be fourteen in a couple months, and I specifically remember you saying only someone who is "fourteen years old or better" couldn't even think about competing in the Arena Cup Tournaments. So if that's the reason we wouldn't meet, you can just forget that right now . . . Or have you forgotten?" Luka says anxiously.

"Of course I haven't forgotten your birthday, and I know at fourteen you're legally able to compete in any real-world competition, but that's not what I meant either. You and I would never compete as opponents because of our classifications. As explained earlier, I am an AD, which means I would compete in the AD Venture Competition, not the Dojakai Monarch Competition," Eiko explains.

"The AD Venture Competition, what's that?" Luka says, too confused to hide his interest.

"Well, in essence, it's a glorified race to the finish comprised of two-man teams. One Runna and one Gunna. The race is a touch-back styled challenge on a living breathing obstacle course where anything goes, and the only rule—well, more like an informal rule—among ADs is, no matter what, you must finish the race. The first Runna to cross the finish line wins it for their team and crew or sponsors. That's it—one winner. There's no second places or runner-ups, but not finishing will get you exiled by the other ADs the brackets. You'll be as good as dead, or wish you was," Eiko describes.

"One Runna and one Gunna, huh? So what's the juice? which one are you?" Luka asks looking him up and down.

"Me, I'm a Runna," Eiko says proudly. "It's the Runna's job to lead his team to victory through some of the deadliest obstacles known to man using only his instinct and quick reflexes to guide them. Sometimes you only have seconds to react while finding the next safest path for you and your team. If the course was a living body, the Runna would be its brain, figuring out the best path of traversal for your success. You have to see the next obstacle before you've even reached it, controlling 'the team's' ranges of motion as one cohesive unit. And if the Runna was the brain, then the Gunna would most definitely be its heart. The Gunna's job is to follow the Runna's lead to a *T*. Balancing 'em, keeping pace with 'em, reacting at a drop of a dime sometimes almost blindly, mimicking their Runna's every reaction to their chosen path, most of the time using only their peripheral vision to do so." Eiko explains.

"Why their peripheral vision?" Andrew asks.

Luka give him a bratty look.

"Because Gunna's do this all while being tasked with one very specific job for their team . . . Which keeping an eye out for any opportunity to eliminate or protect us from opposing team Runnas and Gunnas, by way of peace cannons," Eiko explains.

"Sheesh! Talk about focus. Now I gotta be honest, Unc, you may be a Runna, but even I can sense that it's the Gunnas that gets to have all of the fun," Luka says teasingly.

"I agree, a Runna and Gunna must be completely in sync with one another for the team to have any chance of survival. Enemy Gunnas is only the third worry on the course. Nature's harsh elements all around you and the course itself is what will get you first and second. You have to be able to almost predict your teammate's abilities, and ways of thinking even. The level of trust that a Gunna must have in his Runna is nothing short of the same belief he must have in oxygen keeping him alive. A Gunna's keen sharp eyes and conditioning is really what's most important for the team's success though. Although Gunnas play more of a supportive role, they can still be aggressive and win the race by TKO if they can manage to eliminate all other members of the opposing teams. So yeah, I guess they do get to have a bit more fun than us so to say, yet, everyone knows the real glory of the ADVC is with your Runna crossing the finish line with all ten toes facing down with his AD-Stick in hand and a full breath of oxygen in his lungs," Eiko says convincingly.

"Kinda intense when you say it all dramatic like that, but I gotta say it sounds pretty simple . . . Blast some people, dodge some rocks, spin move pivot and stay warm," Luka says, unimpressed.

"–Simple? Oh, nephew, that's only because you've never seen the course, lil-bro," Eiko says ominously.

"What? Is the finish line inside an active volcano or something?" Luka says teasingly.

"Ha ha, depending on the time of day, yea . . . Tell me, nephew, have you ever heard of the cursed islands of Leveks?" Eiko says dramatically.

Andrew sits up in his seat and begins to pay attention more now.

"The Forbidden Path?" Andrew asks in utter curiousness.

"Mhm. The AD Venture Competition takes place on the Forbidden Path to Leveks, the same path that the Great AD Venture took place on, the same path which claimed the life of the Great AD Kaimen, first of his name only it couldn't claim his glory... not to us. We race to his tomb and back. The five forbidden islands of Leveks, are all scattered throughout the invisible sea but comes together once a year to form the path, one that flips every seven minutes, consistently changing, constantly shifting, reforming, rotating, sinking, and floating. Staying warm is easy, try, one second being in a sandstorm and the next you're surrounded by molted lava made up of the island's core with nothing to stand on, how's that for warm. Tryna keeping your whits about you through that. Do you understand now, Auraluke? It's a race to the finish against all of the elements and Mother Nature herself, and she's always pissed," Eiko says without trying to sound ominous but still comes off that way.

Luka's chair creaks as he leans forward at the edge of his seat.

"So what do you do, bro?" Luka asked, just as interested as his father now.

Eiko glares deeply into Luka's eyes. There is a pause and a silence for a while between them. Suddenly there is a louder creak. Eiko looks over to Andrew, who is in the same pose as Luka, with the same hypnotized look on his face.

"Yeah, bro. What do you do?" Andrew says, completely lost in the sauce.

"You run, you choose a path, and you run your race and hope it leads you to the promised land," Eiko says, as if knowing he will one day die in this race. "There's no way to prepare for it because no two races are ever the same. It's so crazy. Almost fifty percent of the teams that compete will perish running the course, and even now with all this modern technology, no one can predict the algorithm of the Forbidden Path. No one has ever found the keys to its gates. It's the world's greatest mystery, first discovered by the Great AD Kaimen, first of his name, and even he fell to its will, but not before discovering life's second greatest mystery, Dojakai," Eiko says.

"Wait, what?! Hold up, stop bring that back come rewind. So you're telling me you compete in a competition knowing that at least half of you will fall out, for-sure for-sure?" Luka says.

"Ha, it's not for the weak-hearted, I'll say that. I ran it for the first time the year before last. Why do you think I didn't come visit that year or the last one? Zin and I got stranded and left for dead on the fourth island. We crossed the finish line four months after the race was already over, which is normal for the course, but our bodies were so banged up they hospitalized us for another four months after, even with Amey's guidance. There was a point in time I thought we were done for for-sure. The BrixCity Council said the Great AD Kaimen, first of his name, surely must have reached out from the tomb to show us the way home himself. Only I know better. Those four months on those mythodamned islands was pure hell. We had to push ourselves to limits we didn't know our body could even go and beyond, but I knew if we could just make it to the tomb, we would surely find a way back," Eiko says with a dimmed tone. "I knew we could make it, but if it wasn't for Zin, I don't know if I would have found the strength to finish. I wasn't lying when I said I used that secret technique all the time. It was prolly only the second time I was ever genuinely terrified in my life," Eiko says.

"Whoa . . .," Luka says genuinely shocked as he catches a case of the chills.

"Yea.. The tomb of Leveks is the gateway to another world. The path is the bridge from our world to that of the old. This is why the AD's class is suddenly such a prestigious one. According to the father of Dojakai, the only other person to ever pass through the tomb and live to talk about, says our passing on the path honors the Myths, that we should be proud to go out in such a magnificent manner, from the outside looking in I get it but from within, all I could think about was home," Eiko explains.

Luka is glued to Eiko's every word. He imagines all that Eiko describes. Andrew is the first to snap out of it, clearing his throat. Luka snaps out of it too. Eiko notices Andrew shaking his head.

"Whoa, so unreal," Luka gasps with amazement.

Andrew makes a face and moves his head back and forth a few times. Eiko promptly corrects himself.

"Well, that's what the Hystalorian 22.20 course teaches us about the Forbidden Path anyway . . . but no one has gotten the Father of Dojakai to speak on the Hystalorian in years. Who knows what he actually thinks now. But anyway, that wouldn't be your lane, nephew. Trust me, you're an ironclad fighter through and through, a warrior even, you wanna be a Dojakai Handler. You wouldn't have to worry about the cursed course competition, leave that to the Runnas, leave that to me, you fall more into the Handla Brackets if you ask me. It's like I told you before, the Dojakai Monarch Competition is a blood sport for fame, glory, and bragging rights. That's more your speed. That's the tournament you'd be competing in, see it's different," Eiko says.

Andrew seems displeased with the direction of the conversation. He rubs his fingers over his temples, already knowing what's about to occur. Luka sits for a while in silence as he seems to be processing everything. Andrew raises three fingers then drops one, then drops another, then points to Luka with the last finger.

"A Handler?! Wow! so cool, I mean you've never actually given it a name before now. But wow, a Handla, you can really see that by just looking at me Uncle Eiko? I mean I think I can sense it now, What else Eiko? What else do you see? What else do I need to know to become the very best Handler?" Luka says.

"Okay. C'mon, Luka. That's it. I can't take any more of this," Andrew says frustrated now.

"What?!" Luka says, frustrated in his own right.

"What? Really, what?! Are you not seeing what he's doing? Luke, c'mon, be serious for a second. Look how he's talking all ominous and cool sounding, he's just getting you worked up because he knows how much you're into this tournament stuff, he thinks if he convinces you that your a 'Handla', you'll do his dirty work and convince me to send you off to the academy," Andrew says.

"Ok, that's one, because he's a genius! and two because I really am into this tournament stuff and three because he knows I actually can really, really be the very Bes–" Luka says nonchalantly.

"Say it again!" Andrew says, slamming his fist into the table. "Say you really wanna be the very best once more, and my word to the Myths and the stars. I will put you on your back, before the good sun smiles, now I mean that," Andrew says, very slightly humorously. It is almost impossible to tell if he is joking or not. "C'mon, now, heh. Will you let Eiko finish his dinner in peace? Enough of this tournament nonsense. I swear, ever since you told him about this tournament stuff, it's been nonstop with him. He can't even focus on his training anymore. It's ridiculous," Andrew fusses.

"It's okay, Andrew, training is only physical. I want him to have the mental edge on the rest of the other kids next year. Besides, you're the one that brought up his daydreams about the tournament circuits. It's only right I set Auraluke straight?," Eiko says.

"Reduke-snay on the Auraluke-snay." Luka says but is ignored.

"Yeah, but I didn't meant–" Andrew starts.

"Ah-Ahht! it was your idea—" Eiko interrupts.

"But seriously, the very veries though—" Andrew jumps back in.

"Eh-eh-ehht! he's eager that's good—" Eiko finalizes.

Andrew shuts up and pouts, mumbling to himself.

"Okay. Now, Luke. Remember, to compete at tournament level in any class, you'll need something first, and that something is . . . ?!" Eiko says, showing the most enthusiasm he's had all night.

"An AD-Stick!" Luka shouts, jumping up onto his seat, throwing his head back, and pointing up to the sky.

"No!" Andrew and Eiko both blurt out. "Do you see what I deal with every day?" Andrew adds.

"No I get it, seriously Auraluke, this is the world we live in, at least act like you're from the land," Eiko says.

Luka seems lost.

"Dojakai! I'm talking about Dojakai bro. All competitors needs at least one Dojakai to support them in the circuits. That's tournament rule number one. Got it!" Eiko says.

"But Eiko, you don't have any Dojakai?" Luka says, surprised.

"That's only because I chose not to accept the one the academy offered me. Zin uses a stand-in for our team, but it's only ever gotten in the way, probably the reason we got stranded out there to begin with. Nah, I'd much rather it just be me, Zin, and my best friend here for now," Eiko says proudly.

Eiko pats his AD-Stick on the side of his hip. Andrew isn't convinced.

"Cool, I can sense it, but I've never even seen a Dojakai close up in real life before, Dad still keeps me home training when he runs out for resources," Luka says.

"Ha ha. Never seen a Dojakai . . . This kid is wild," Eiko says, amused and unconvinced.

Everyone else becomes extremely serious.

"Wait, seriously, Andrew, he's almost fourteen years old, you're in a Burg-less jungle surrounded by nothing but land beasts for 'feeding our kids well'," Eiko says defiantly.

"That's because Dojakai are very dangerous and unpredictable. It's not like they're just walking around smiling at humans, saying, 'Hi, I'm a Dojakai. Pet me.' You have to be able to read the nature of these feral beasts. Dojakai are nature's correction to the nature of us. If you know that, then you have to behave accordingly when in the presence of one. You must know how to keep your composure, Dojakai are extremely sensitive. They feel very differently from you and I, son. So no, not yet," Andrew argues.

"Dad hates Dojakai," Luka whispers out loud.

"No, I never said that. There's a lot of beautifully majestic Dojakai in this world, only I lived long enough to know what some Dojakai are capable of," Andrew claims.

"You're living in the past, Andrew. I know you old-timers had it hard, with the Great Wars and all, but we've come a long way since then. For one, we have D-Shooters now. Dojakai no longer have the free will to betray us or act aggressive toward us anymore. And as far as 'feral' ones go, most of these lands has nearly been wiped clean of the powerful more bestial Dojakai. The Amazin' Eights made sure of that . . . Nowadays, the only way to even see any Dojakai feral or otherwise is by way of academy, Arena Circuits, or I don't know by like accidentally wandering into a KaiZoo or something, but no one is ignorant enough to wander into a Kai—" Eiko says.

Eiko talks, simultaneously turning to Luka who is staring at him with a big goofy smile, nodding his head.

"Well, most people aren't that ignorant," Eiko says, uncertain of Luka's level of understanding.

"What's a KaiZoo, is that a competition too...?" Luka asks.

"—My point in the flesh," Andrew chimes in abruptly.

"No, It's an area of land where known untouched Dojakai like to congregate. There's one not far from here actually," Eiko says leaning back looking towards the window.

"What is he talking about Pop-Rock. . . There's no Dojakai around here . . . right... Dad?" Luka claims trying to cover up his nervousness.

"There used to be, but I think they've all migrated away from here," Andrew says, looking away from Eiko.

"He's probably right, there isn't many KaiZoo' left, but the biggest one can still be found in the center of Penyow. It's common sense nowadays to know which boroughs harbor the world's most dangerous Dojakai in one habitat, ones that couldn't be held. I remember The Academy took us all—the whole bracket, on a field trip there once, weeding out the would-be dropouts early I guess, I sense it though, couldn't have their weakness bringing the entire units moral down ya know. Let's just say not everyone made it back that day," Eiko says ominously.

"Good riddance," Luka subjectively adds.

Shadows of creatures with red eyes haunted Eiko's thoughts. He shakes it off.

"Disgusting, there was a time Dojakai could roam free, although it was brief, there was a time we co-existed. Why aren't they teaching that in your Hystalorian 22.20's or whatever? Just look, this is exactly what I've been telling you, son. D-Shooters, KaiZoo', Arena Circuits, Tournaments, and is anybody speaking up? No! The original members of the Amazin' Eights should've done better, And the BrixCity Council isn't any better," Andrew states.

Eiko stares at Andrew for a while sharing a look. Everyone is silent.

"Well! Um, I think that's my cue. Thanks for dinner, but, I think I'ma head out. Zin thinks I'm on a mental retreat I told him I'd link up with him when I got back."

Eiko gets up from the table.

"What! You're leaving, you can't leave yet! Eiko! You just got here! I haven't seen you in forever. How else am I supposed to learn what I need to know to be the very very best Handler—" Luka says.

Andrew glares at him, a mighty stare of all stares.

"Hehe gotcha, Pop-star," Luka says double hand pointing while winking and clicking twice with his mouth.

Andrew moves swiftly toward him around the table and everything goes blank. Luka is suddenly standing up rubbing his head from a slight daze.

"Fine, but that one was worth it. It's just academy kids get to have so much fun, making friends, chasing clout and holding Dojakai. Why does my life have to suck so bad? Why can't I go to BrixCity Academy with Uncle Eiko? Why do I have to be homeschooled?" Luka says disappointed.

"Ha ha haa, you two are nuts, he he. C'mon, lil-bro, I'll see you again before you know it. Remember stay senses-flat you'll know how I'm coming. Besides it'll be the Summer Chalices soon. School's almost out, they're going to announce the new BrixCity sanctions in a few days, if they haven't already. If I'm not there to welcome the new inductees. It'll look weird for me not to show up," Eiko says, adjusting the chain around his arm. "But don't worry I'll see you at the academy next year uh? Uh?" Eiko says joking and bumping his elbow into Luka while staring at Andrew trying to convince him.

Luka looks up at Eiko proudly, unable to help himself from releasing his huge goofy smiles. Eiko lets out a small smirk then gets up and walks toward the door.

"Hey, uh let me walk you out, little brother," Andrew says promptly.

Andrew and Eiko walk to the door. Luka is still rubbing his head disappointed, when he looks over at Eiko's plate noticing he never ate a single bite. Luka is confused as he looks back at Eiko walking out, but then looks back at the plate again, he shrugs and slides it in front of his seat then smiles.

Ignorance Is Bliss

...Luka's house, Inside their dining room,

A short time has passed and Luka is sitting there with two empty plates in front of him. He seems satisfied. He starts to faintly hear voices coming from just outside the window closest to the front door. Luka sneaks up to the window without being seen. He sees Eiko is still there talking to Andrew on the front porch.

"{Hm . . . Still here? Eiko must be going toe-to-toe with Dad, trying to convince him register me into the academy next year,}" Luka thinks. "He's so cool!" Luka says out loud and has to duck thinking he was heard.

Eiko looks at the window but doesn't notice him. Luka continues to try and eavesdrop but can barely hear what they are saying. Andrew and Eiko seem to be locked in a serious conversation.

Ignorance is Bliss: Scene

...Luka's house, Outside on the porch.

"Now do you understand everything I've just said?" Andrew says finally.

"I'm not a child anymore, Andrew. I understand things the first time I'm told," Eiko says back coherently.

Eiko just stares at Andrew intensely.

"One last thing, about your friend, this . . . Zin? He doesn't actually know . . . ?" Andrew says cautiously.

"–I know your rules, Andrew. You guys are still good up here. He only knows what he needs to know. I'll handle everything that's important to you," Eiko says firmly.

Andrew looks at Eiko pleasantly, then looks off into the dark sky and up at the bright crescent moon. Eiko slowly follows his lead.

"It came around so quick this year, hasn't it? Auraluke's birthday . . . and Lusa's . . .," Andrew says unable to finish.

"–Don't . . .," Eiko says abruptly, serious.

"–Eiko, you have to had at least learned to talk about it by now. It's okay to talk about her, to say her name even. You know Auraluke would much rather be called by his nickname. You won't even say it because it's similarity to Lu–to Lusibelle's nickname, Lusa. Little brother, I hoped you could move past it. It's been fourteen years since . . .," Andrew says.

"And I said don't," Eiko says, turning to Andrew in anger.

"Look, I know you two were close, little brother," Andrew begins.

"Close?! Did you really just say the word 'close' to me? She wasn't some friend or Dojakai. She was my sister! My strength and legacy," Eiko says, becoming even more angry.

"And she was my wife! You don't think I've grieved! You don't think I've ...felt," Andrew says but gets choked up. "Look, I loved your family, I loved your sister, but this, this family, right here, right now, the ones who are still here with us, that young man in there, he is just as much apart of you legacy as he is mine. Little brother, she was my strength too . . .," Andrew says, becoming slightly emotional.

"And had she not been, she'd might still be alive, they'd all be, or have you forgotten that part too ol-timer? . . . And for the record, I am not your little brother. We are not family Andrew. I have no family anymore because of you," Eiko says emotionless.

"I understand how you feel about me," Andrew says, correcting his emotions. "But you still have Luke. He is your flesh and blood. That is your sister's legacy in there, he still has the blood of your father, his grandfather running through his veins. Perishable or not you both share a legacy," Andrew says, there is an awkward pause, Andrew sighs. "Look, all I'm saying is that you don't have to keep so many different emotions bottled up inside you that way. Love, anger, pain, grief, regret.. Revenge?" Andrew says reluctantly. "That kind of combination of emotions would cause even the happiest man the most terrible suffering," Andrew says with understanding.

"You have, no idea," Eiko says vengefully. "And by Myths and Retrokai, I swear that when the time comes, I am going to repay all of my suffering back, tenfold. You know me, Andrew, the real me, that weird happy kid, someone who didn't get it. You know, I didn't choose this path for myself, It was chosen for me. But even so, I will run this path at my best. By the Myths, the Hystalorian and the Great AD Kaimen, first of his name as my witness I will finish this race with all my strength intact. What other choice is there, right?" Eiko says ominously still.

Eiko has revenge in his eyes. There's another pause between them.

"Hey, regardless of what, I do owe you a thanks," Andrew says.

Eiko sits in his pause, but he looks up at Andrew who seems pleasant.

". . . For what?" Eiko asks.

"For being the way you are with him, despite everything else. He really looks up to you, perhaps more than he does me. I know you sense it too," Andrew says amusingly.

Andrew and Eiko are stuck in a short pause for a third time. Eiko can't help but lighten up, slightly smiling to himself.

"Tuh. He's such a weird kid though. Hehe, happy though . . . But so weird," Eiko looks up at Andrew. "You're wrong though, you know that, right?" Eiko says.

"What do you mean?" Andrew asks confused.

"About Auraluke, about what you said earlier, he doesn't lack courage . . . focus, maybe, but courage, not in the slightest. It's you—you're pushing him too hard. You can't sense it but I can. Courage, he has tons of, he gets that from Bells. It's something else," Eiko says.

Andrew listens attentively. Luka finally manages to open the window as silently as possible to hear what they are saying more clearly. They don't notice.

"If you ask me he's weak. Too weak to be ready for anything this world will throw at him," Eiko says deliberately.

The window closes slowly and quietly.

"He lacks faith, faith in himself, faith in his abilities, and faith in the abilities of those around him here. He's strong but he's weak for his age, in here," Eiko says fiercely to Andrew.

Eiko puts his fist to his chest then points his pinky finger and taps his head.

"The sooner you realize that, the sooner you'd let me do what needs to be done. Let me take him with me to BrixCity where he can receive an organized education and a chance to be a part of the new world. Your problem is you can't see past your own experiences, and now neither can he. You needed someone to understand you and your choices, so badly that you unknowingly forced him to carry your burdens as well. He needs a breath of fresh air. He needs to get out of here like now," Eiko says without remorse.

"And I guess that would mean you would look after him, is that right? And what makes you think your burdens are any easier to carry than mine. What makes you think your way is so much better than mine, is it your fancy clothes or your shiny equipment. No, he comes outside every day and breaths the freshest air right where he belongs, at home," Andrew says in defense.

"You're so stuck you don't even get it, not outside—out of this place, out of this jungle, into the new open world. He's never even seen a Dojakai. Andrew, a Dojakai? And this jungle is flooded with them, are you serious? You think you're helping him but really you're hindering him. You raised him right, congratulations, be proud of that. Have some pride in your abilities as a parent to let him go out there and apply what you've taught him. If he goes out and makes the wrong choices, let him learn from his own mistakes firsthand for not listening to you. It isn't right to force him to see what you want him to see secondhand too. Otherwise a few inappropriate words in vain will be the least of your worries. You can't keep him locked away forever, sooner or later, it won't matter, sooner or later he will figure things out. It's just a matter of time," Eiko says, sure of himself.

"Eiko, we've spoke about this. It's too—"Andrew says.

"What?! Dangerous? And that is exactly why you are in this position now. You ran from your problems and you brought them here!—to me!—And my family!!" Eiko says becoming almost livid but immediately catches himself and exhales. "And yet, the path is already set," Eiko says calmly. "An ever-changing, rotating, shifting, floating, sinking race we call life." Eiko says with no added emotion at all (sighing). "C'mon, Andrew, just go with the flow for once in your life. You can't control everything at all times, bro. You of all people should know life doesn't work like that," Eiko says convincingly.

Andrew smirks while Eiko smiles innocently at him.

"You sense me?" Eiko says jokingly, Andrew chuckles to himself a bit.

As soon as he turns his back to him, Eiko's expression becomes serious and he looks back at the house through the corner of his eye then toward the forest he came from. Without another word being said, he runs off into the dark open field and into jungle. Andrew pauses for a moment until he is completely out of sight, then begins to shake his head. When he turns around, he sees the window is cracked open and curtains are blowing from the draft. Andrew shakes his head again, stretches, wipes his face, and walks back in pleasantly.

"So, seconds?! Or should I be saying fourth? Hey! I wasn't finished with that," Andrew says in distress.

"Nope. Move ya feet lose ya seat!" Luka calls.

Diss is Bliss

Eiko runs not far from the house when he runs into Zin, who is leaning on a tree waiting for him. Zin unfolds his arms and stretches a deep stretch, yawning.

"M'Thodamn's blush. That's gotta be the longest 'twenty minutes tops' I ever experienced in my life haha, but, anyway, how'd it go, bro?" Zin says aggressively.

Zin hands him his A.D-Stick

"Just as I expected. The old-timer's as stubborn as ever, but never too far off his game. The plan stays the same for now, especially if we're going to get rid of 'em. We wait for the signs and then we make our move. It's simple. In the meantime, we'll need to make a public statement before the chalices. Zin. There can be no room for mistake copy?" Eiko says even more aggressively.

"The loss of a one's parent can cause a lot of suffering in a guy's heart, I can't imagine how you felt when you lost both parents and your sister all in one night to that palm-gripping filth. I don't have any doubts, but I need to hear you say that you are sure about this..." Zin asks genuinely.

"Hm?" Eiko grunts.

"Do you really think this plan will work, I mean, this is BrixCity we're talking about Beha?" Zin says as solid as ever.

Eiko grabs him, shoving him into the tree he was leaning on. Eiko has a near crazed look in his eyes.

"Zin, after this, my nephew will never be my nephew again. The plan must be perfect, there better not be no doubts. You feel me, Beha?!" Eiko says aggressively.

Eiko lets him go then looks away, realizing he's gone too far.

"Sorry," Eiko says quickly.

"No, I get it, brother, you are my brother, I haven't forgotten that, but you should already know without questioning my loyalty that I'm with you, Beha." Zin says aggressively.

Zin looks at Eiko strongly holding his chin high. Eiko holds his expression unwaveringly until he finally raising his chin equally as high. Zin smiles then grabs the side of Eiko's head and leans in and clanks the side of their chins together. There is a pause of respect for one another. Then without any cues, Eiko turns and runs off into the dark night. Zin jerks his head up then runs behind him.

The sun rises on Luka's house. The sun shines brightly reflecting its glare off the top of two mountains that are side by side in the distance from Luka's house. The peak of the mountain shines brightly over Kayuga, illuminating the entire jungle. Luka and Andrew are in the same spot they started in before. Luka yawns.

"Good Morning! No slacking or wocky space-outs today, okay?! I expect you at your best. You hear me, Luke?!"

Luka yawns again and nods his head waiving his hand gesturing for Andrew to calm down, he feels awkward.

"Okay fine, let's begin," Andrew says swiftly.

Andrew immediately takes off, running out of Luka's view. Luka is surprised by his speed but instantly becomes alert and takes off running after him.

uka and Andrew run side by side. Andrew scoops up a handful of small rocks without losing momentum or slowing down.

He begins throwing them one by one at Luka, he ducks each of them acrobatically, clearly trying to mimic the flashy movements he seen from Eiko. The rocks whistles through the air at Luka. Suddenly, three more significantly larger rocks come flying Luka's way at the same time. He dodges them, diving out of the way of them all, changing his direction as soon as he lands from running with Andrew to running directly at him.

Seeing his opening Luka jumps again, this time throwing a kick at his father but misses, Andrew smirks, continuing his pace and speed. Luka lands and again gives chase. They both continue to run through the forest by their house, eventually leading to what appears to be a manmade obstacle course. Luka marvels at the obstacle course for a split second slightly slowing in stride. He smiles to himself then starts to pick up speed the closer he gets to it.

Andrew comes flying at him from out of nowhere delivering a devastating knee to Luka's ribs with tremendous force.

"Not good enough!" Andrew blurts out aggressively.

Luka is sent flying back.

"Nothing is new in this world. Notice everything as if you already expected it to be. Do this and nothing will ever shock you enough to distract you! Stay true," Andrew says thunderingly.

Luka is soaring back, finally just about to hit the floor...

I'm proud of you: Scene

. . . The sun is setting on the open field

Luka hits the floor in the open field, in front of their house. He tumbles backward, bouncing off of the floor a few times, eventually regaining control, flipping backwards on to his feet while continuing to slide backwards.

He has to dig his hand in the dirt to slow himself down to a stop, but as soon as he looks up in the direction from which he was sent flying from, he is met with a fireball an quickly dives out of the way. There is a burning patch of grass on his shoulder but, he isn't effected by it because he is wearing a body suit that protects his skin from the elements. He grabs the flame and throws it to the floor, it immediately disperses.

"Bro?!!" Luka says exhausted.

"I'm not your bro! Now defend!" Andrew says.

Luka poses in a stance, determined to get it right. Andrew is sitting in their tractor across the field, of what looks to be a mechanic beast, rumbling with smoking coming out of it as it slowly creeps towards him...

I'm proud of you: Scene

...A gloomy day, Luka's training grounds

Suddenly another fireball comes flying his way. He dodges it, but more follow. He begins running, ducking, and twirling, eventually spinning around acrobatically, avoiding being hit by the flames, determined to reach Andrew. He dodges more flurries of rapid-fire attacks the closer he gets to him. Finally, Andrew shoots one that Luka is forced to dive out of the way of, and as soon as he recovers to his feet, he flexes toward Andrew with pride.

"Ha!" Luka taunts.

And is met with a front kick to the chest for boasting.

"Always keep your attention on your immediate enemy no matter what else is going on around you, understood? Keep your guard up and your senses flat when in a clash of wills. Be alert enough that you can make an adjustment at any moment, but fluid enough that you can switch from defense to delivering an offensive game changer to your enemy in an instant. Be better!" Andrew says, firmly still unsatisfied.

Luka is still stumbling back from the power of Andrew's kick when he finally catches his balance.

I'm proud of you: Scene

...Kayuga Territory, Luka's Beach

He immediately turns to Andrew who is already punching him in the face with so much force that the sweat from his forehead flies off of his head in slow motion. His sweat droplets soars through the air toward the ground. More blows are thrown at him in the background as he immediately begins blocking them.

"Show me your offense, Fight back!" Andrew screams in the background.

I'm proud of you: Scene

...Luka's Valley, Open fields

The sweat droplets hits the grass one by one, and a lot more come after that until Luka can be seen doing intense push-ups. Sweat drips from his face as he strains to do more, you can see each muscle as they rip and each vein as they pop on his arms, neck, and body. There is a huge tree log strapped to his back.

"Fi... fi– fifty," Luka says trembling.

Luka strains to push up, but thrusts his arms forward, locking his elbows and holding them in place. His chest and back begins to flex tighten up until finally his elbows unlock. He falls face first into a puddle of his own sweat, causing a small splash!

I'm proud of you: Scene

...Luka's beach, Fog takes the skies on a windy day,

Luka splashes into the ocean as it slowly begins to rain. Andrew swims through the ocean, heavy waves crashes into him. The rain begins to pick up even more, but Andrew is swimming through the waves with ease. He looks back and doesn't see Luka. Andrew stops and begins looking around for Luka with concern.

"Luke?!" Andrew twists around.

Andrew sees a huge wave coming his way when he is suddenly yanked underwater. Luka lets go of his leg and swims gracefully into his view. Luka is smiling at him underwater. He looks angry at first but slowly releases a goofy smile back. A strong current swooshes past both of their faces again as they swim off.

I'm proud of you: Scene

...Luka's house, Training circle – On a dark thundering night

Andrew stands across from Luka in the combat circle in the field of their home. A few leaves blow in the wind from a nearby cedar tree to the combat circle and is met with a few leaves from the forest. The orange stringy petals and green leaves begin to dance with each other around them. Andrew begins running along the edge of the combat circle. Luka begins moving in the same direction. Both are running in the same circular pattern. They both begin to move toward each other while running in the same circular pattern until finally they meet in the middle.

Luka jumps throwing a flying kick. Andrew blocks it then throws two heavy punches of his own. Luka blocks them, both attacks bouncing off his lean arms. Luka quickly ducks catching Andrew off guard and sweeps at his feet hooking one. Andrew loses his balance nearly stumbling out of the combat circle.

Ha Ha

Good job, son, I'm proud of you!

Luka runs in to attack, when Andrew quickly regains his balance, using the boarded edge of the fighting circle then jumps back into him throwing a powerful straight kick. Luka isn't surprised, his head is lowered, his eyes are focused on Andrew's body movements, he sees it coming. He side-steps the strong kick, turns, and steps off Andrew knee and simultaneously back kicks Andrew in the chest with tremendous force. Then follows it up with a second back kick with his other leg, twisting around further and twisting double leg drop kicks Andrew in his abdomen, all before hitting the ground. Andrew falls flat on his back outside of the circle. Andrew grabs his stomach in pain but quickly looks back up at Luka, who is already standing over him in his fighting stance. Andrew is a bit shocked but pleased. He sits up, smiles and nods.

I'm proud of you: Scene

...Luka's House, backyard – Sun rises on a peaceful day,

Luka and Andrew sits on a log in the back of their house on the cliff overlooking the beach below. They watch the sun set while eating a sandwich. They are talking. Luka is laughing and seems to be acting out a fight, probably from a recent daydream. Andrew begins to laughs a huge laugh as well and puts his arm over Luka. It makes Luka happy to see his father genuinely tuned in to his story.

"Good job, son, I'm proud of you . . . But you still not ready." Andrew says.

Luka falls off of the log he's sitting on head first to the ground in confused disbelief.

Auraluke

"I know, I know, not what you was expecting right, plus it's like "Oh–oh, I thought you were gonna jump through a window. What happened to that part?" And you're right, I did but nah, son, we ain't there yet. I told you I'd start you somewhere in the beginning, this was just a little before my fourteenth birthday, right before everything changed. I needed you to know what my life was like before all of the madness happened. I needed you to understand where I was coming from. Only then will you truly understand why I made all the choices I made leading up to that moment, and so much more. Mythics! If you're reading this right now, then you either know one of two things, one nothing is what I thought it was or Two, I'm probably gonna get caught lacking in this new world and the people here are probably going to try and end me. If you are reading this right now, I need you to tell everyone it wasn't supposed to be like this but even so, tell them thank you. Thank you for teaching me what it meant to be a part of the amazin' world of Dojakai. You sense me. Truly hers . . . Auraluke." Luka narrates.

...More is soon to come.

V.01